It's My Birthday... Finally!
A Leap Year Story

D1416107

Michelle Whitaker Winfrey

It's My Birthday... Finally!
A Leap Year Story

Illustrations by Joyce M. Turley
Dixon Cove Design

Hobby House Publishing Group, Inc.
P.O. Box 1527
Jackson, NJ 08527

ISBN: 978-0-9727179-5-3

Library of Congress Control Number: 2007932123

Frog carrying mushroom with or without the double H is a
Trademark of Hobby House Publishing Group, Inc.

Printed in the United States of America

Dedicated to the memory of
Aunt Mamie
February 29, 1912 – February 27, 2007

For Miles Phillip Winfrey
Born February 29, 1992

Edited by Jeannette Cézanne
Customline Wordware, Inc.
www.customline.com

Contents

It's My Birthday... Finally!
A Leap Year Story

Foreword
By Warren F. White Jr., Principal

For the past thirty years I have been a public school teacher, guidance counselor, vice-principal and presently principal of a large urban middle school, where over twenty-three languages are spoken in my classrooms. I recognize and applaud the uniqueness of all students. There are many personal and societal challenges children face while seeking acceptance by their peers and adults. As the parent of two sons I have watched them develop their own versatility and commonalities on their own.

In this book, *It's My Birthday... Finally! A Leap Year Story,* the reader meets eight-year-old Miles, who was born on February twenty-ninth. Miles's family, friends and classmates approach this special birthday celebration from very different points of view, and their teacher seizes the moment. Mrs. Garcia is a caring, compassionate person. She recognizes the hurt on Miles's face when he is being teased by his classmates.

They say he is two years old, not eight like the rest of the class! Mrs. Garcia grasps this opportunity to accentuate the positive and eliminate the negative by capitalizing on the students' natural curiosity. She skillfully redirects their enthusiasm. Drawing on history, mathematics, and mythology to investigate the origins of Leap Year, Mrs. Garcia exposes her students to a lesson in life.

The author, Michelle Winfrey, uses a humanistic approach throughout the story. The reader learns a very valuable lesson: celebrate uniqueness – it's a great way to approach life. The book is filled with factual information about leap years, calendars, and history.

Introduction
How old will Miles be?

Just three more days and Miles finally has a birthday!
A big celebration has been planned.

First, he's having a party at school. His mom is baking a cake for his class. Then Miles is going out to dinner with his parents and two best friends. On Saturday, Miles is having a grand birthday party with friends, grandparents, aunts, uncles and cousins.

Finally, after waiting four years, Miles has a birthday! Miles Thomas Phillips was born February 29, 1992. That makes him very special. That makes him a Leap Year Day child. When Miles turned four he did not understand what this meant. But now that he is going to be eight, he realizes that his birthday only comes once every four years!

So, how old will Miles really be … eight, or two?

Thursday, February 27

Thirty days hath September,
April, June and November;
All the rest have thirty-one
Save February, she alone
Hath eight days and a score
Til Leap Year gives her one day more.

– Author Unknown

Chapter 1
The ride to school

"Good morning, Mama!" exclaimed Miles on Thursday, February twenty-seventh, as he entered the kitchen. Miles was wearing his favorite navy blue pants and character shirt with sneakers. As always, he had on a baseball cap with his braided ponytail coming out the back. His tail is so long, he can wrap it around his neck. The rest of his black hair is cut very short with just a hint of curls on top.

"Good morning! What would you like for breakfast?" his mom asked.

"Nothing," said Miles. "I'm too excited to eat. Tomorrow is my party at school, and Saturday's finally my birthday!"

"Yes, it is, but today you need your breakfast. How about some blueberry waffles?" Blueberry waffles are Miles's favorite.

"Okay, I'll have two." Miles loves blueberry waffles covered with butter and syrup. His dog Einstein loves them, too. He gets to eat the leftovers. When Miles is home, Einstein is always near him. Sometimes they think that Einstein should have been called Shadow.

While Mrs. Phillips made his waffles, Miles looked at the mountain of large goody bags for his friends at school. They were piled high on the table like a pyramid, with the blue ones for the boys on the bottom, and the pink ones for the girls on top. Miles and his mom went to the party store on Saturday to buy all the items for the goody bags. Each goody bag had a cup, two pencils, and lots of candy, a small note pad, and a game.

Yesterday after school Miles helped his mom put them together. Each goody bag was tied with red curly string. They even made one for his teacher, Mrs. Garcia.

"My friends are really going to love their goody bags," said Miles.

"Yes, they are," his mom replied as she handed him his breakfast plate.

While Miles ate, Mrs. Phillips packed his lunch and snack. She reminded him that she would pick him up after school.

When she was done, they talked about how much fun they had putting the goody bags together. At seven-thirty, the school bus arrived.

"The bus is here! Get your school bag and lunch box," his mom said. "And don't forget your jacket!"

After many hugs and kisses, Miles finally boarded the bus for school. As usual, Einstein watched Miles get on the bus through the front door, his tail a-wagging.

As Miles got on the bus, he looked for his best friend John.

"Over here, Miles!" John yelled from the middle of the bus. John saved a seat for Miles. John is four months older than Miles, but they are exactly the same size. In fact, they are so much alike that they could be brothers. John was also wearing a character shirt, and his blond hair was spiked with gel. They have been friends since they were four years old.

"Boy, I guess you're excited about tomorrow and Saturday?" John asked.

"Yeah, I didn't sleep at all last night," Miles answered through a yawn. "I helped my mom make the goody bags after school yesterday, and today she is baking a cake for our class tomorrow."

"You're lucky," said Sean, who was sitting behind Miles and John. "My birthday comes every year, so it's no big deal, just another birthday. But yours comes on Leap Year Day, that's way cool." Sean has been friends with Miles and John since the first grade. Sean was already eight like John. His birthday was during the summer.

Just then Karen yelled from the back of the bus "Miles will be two years old on Saturday!"

"Karen has a big mouth," Miles whispered to John, scowling.

"It's loud, too!" said John.

"Miles will be two years old on Saturday!" Karen yelled again. Miles frowned. He will be eight, not two. He has waited his whole life to be eight. Several of the other kids started to sing, "Miles will be two! Miles will be two!"

Miles yelled back, "I will be eight, not two!"

"Don't let it bother you," said John. "They are just jealous. They wish they were born on Leap Year Day."

23

"I know, but I'm *not* going to be two. I am going to be eight!" For the rest of the ride to school, Miles tried to ignore the singing. *It's going to be a long day,* Miles thought. He was glad that he had his friends John and Sean with him.

Calendar Facts

The earth's year is 365.24219 days long. That's how long it takes the Earth to make one rotation around the sun, and through the seasons. But until Julius Caesar proclaimed every fourth year a **leap year**, calendars were a mess. If you lived long enough, you could experience your birthday in two or three different seasons! This was the *Julian calendar.*

In 45 BC, Emperor Julius Caesar proclaimed the last day of February as Leap Year Day, skipping it three out of four years. Back then, February 30th was the last day of the month of the year, which is why he picked it.

In 4 AD, Emperor Augustus Caesar corrected a counting error in leap years. He also got the month of August named after him, and stole the last day of February so that August can have 31 days, just like Julius's month. Now February has 29 days in a leap year.

In 1582, Pope Gregory XIII moved the end of the year to December 31st, and made century years leap years if they are divisible by 400. By moving the end of the year back two months, Easter now occurs in the spring.

This is the *Gregorian calendar* that we follow today.

When the *Gregorian calendar* was first implemented, it caused a great uproar throughout the Roman Catholic world, because it required the deduction of thirteen days in order to bring the calendar back into line with the seasons. Many people rioted in the streets, thinking that these days had somehow been deducted from their lives!

The *Gregorian calendar* is now used throughout most of the world, the most famous exceptions being the Greek and Russian Orthodox Churches, which still observe the old *Julian Calendar.*

Chapter 2
A Leap Year lesson

Finally they arrived at school. Miles and his friends hurried off the bus and into the building. Jackson Hillside Elementary School is a beautiful red brick building with lots of windows. There are basketball courts, soccer fields, baseball fields and a special area to play jump rope and hopscotch.

Miles and his friends entered their large blue-and-white classroom. Their teacher, Mrs. Garcia, greeted them with a big smile and said "good morning" to every student as he or she arrived.

Mrs. Garcia has short black wavy hair that she wears pulled behind her ears, and she always has on a sweater. Today her sweater was black with pearl buttons to match the black-and-white dress she was wearing. The class gave her this sweater for her birthday. Last month the class counted eighteen different sweaters worn by Mrs. Garcia. Of course, she doesn't know that they counted them.

"Good morning, Mrs. Garcia," the kids all said as they entered the room. Mrs. Garcia noticed that they were a bit rambunctious today.

The first part of the morning was used to review homework. Once that was done, Mrs. Garcia always gave them a five-minute break. During today's break she once again noticed that they were a little extra excited.

"Okay, settle down," Mrs. Garcia said. "I have a special lesson planned today. We are going to learn about leap year."

"What is there to learn?" Bobby asked. Bobby sits in the front of the class and always has a question, no matter what the subject is.

"Yeah, we already know that it comes once every four years on February twenty-ninth," added Mary.

"And we know that Miles will be two years old on Saturday, because he was born on February twenty-ninth!" yelled Karen from her seat in the back. Several of the kids started to laugh. Miles put his head down. He was *not* going to be two! He was going to be eight! Mrs. Garcia noticed Miles's lowered head. But she did not say anything.

"Well, does anyone know why February only has twenty-eight days, and one extra day every four years?" Mrs. Garcia looked around the room. No hands were up. "Well, that is what we are going to learn today."

For the rest of the morning they learned about the *Thoth* calendar, which was invented in Egypt five thousand years ago. They learned about the ancient Roman calendar and how Julius Caesar developed a different calendar. Mrs. Garcia also explained how Julius Caesar took a day from February in order to make his birth month longer. Then, after Julius Caesar died, Augustus Caesar, his nephew, had the calendar changed again by renaming the month in which his uncle was born. Augustus also took another day from February and changed his birth month so that it would have thirty-one days, just like his uncle's.

Mrs. Garcia went on to explain how the names of the twelve months in our calendar and the names of the

days in those months came about. "Can anyone guess which months are named for Julius and Augustus Caesar?"

Several hands went up. Mrs. Garcia picked Carmen.

"July for Julius and August for Augustus," answered Carmen.

"That's right," said Mrs. Garcia. "Originally, July was called Quintillis and August was called Sextilis."

"So that gives us 28 days," commented Bobby. "But why do we have 29 days every four years?"

"Does everyone remember the lesson we had last week about how the earth rotates around the sun?" Several hands went up. Mrs. Garcia called on Sally.

"It takes 365 and a quarter days to complete the rotation," Sally answered.

"Correct. Now let's use our fractions to figure this out. If it takes 365¼ days to complete the rotation that means that we have ..."

"One extra day every four years!" shouted Miles.

"That's right," Mrs. Garcia said. The lesson was fascinating and lasted all morning. Miles was particularly happy about this. Perhaps everyone, especially Karen, would forget that Saturday is only his second real birthday!

"So, as you can see, February is a very special month and February 29 is even more special," said Mrs. Garcia. Just then the lunch bell rang.

"Think about this during lunch. We will finish this afternoon."

A Lesson about Thoth

In ancient Egyptian mythology, *Thoth* was the god of the moon, the god of wisdom, the measurer of time, and the inventor of writing and numbers.

Shu (shoe), the son of the sun god, Re (ray), reigned as king of Egypt for many years. When his daughter Nut (newt) fell in love with the god Geb (gebb), Shu was wildly jealous. To keep the lovers far apart, he turned Nut into the sky and Geb into the earth. Then he cursed Nut with barrenness, proclaiming that there were no months of the year in which she could give birth.

Thoth, the god of the moon, time and measure, took pity on Nut and Geb. He challenged the reigning gods to a game of dice and beat them all soundly. As his prize, he asked the gods to give him five days in addition to those that already existed. Thoth in turn presented the five extra days to the sky goddess, Nut. Because these five extra days did not belong to any particular month, they did not fall under Shu's curse. Thus, the goddess was able to use them to produce five children, including Osiris (oh-SIGH-rus) and Isis (EYE-sus).

Prior to Thoth's gift, each of the twelve months of the Egyptian calendar had 30 days, resulting in a 360-day year. Thoth's act of kindness reconciled the Egyptian calendar with the earth's actual 365-day cycle.

Thoth had many roles. In addition to being the god of the moon, the god of wisdom, and the measurer of time, he was scribe, moralist, messenger, and supreme magician. The ancient Egyptians credited him with inventing writing. He was the patron god of all arts, sciences, and intellectual pursuits. Ancient Egyptians believed that before the dead could enter the Afterworld, their hearts were weighed against a feather of truth to determine whether they had led good and honest lives. In his role as scribe, Thoth recorded the results of each judgment.

Chapter 3
Miles is not too happy

During lunch, Miles overheard some of the kids talking about the morning lesson, and his Leap Year Day birthday. *Why can't they talk about something else?* he wondered. Every once in a while someone would say the word *two* and then there would be laughter.

"Just ignore it," said Sean.

"Yeah, don't let it get to you," followed John.

"You don't understand," Miles said sadly, pushing his lunch aside. He had suddenly lost his appetite.

While eating her lunch in the teachers' lounge, Mrs. Garcia mentioned to Mr. Jones, the assistant principal, that Miles seemed to get upset when someone mentioned that he would be two on Saturday. "Well, when he's forty, he'll appreciate being ten," Mr. Jones said with a laugh.

"Yeah, but for now, he's going to be eight and wants to be called eight," Mrs. Garcia replied. "Somehow, I've got to tell the class that this bothers Miles, without him knowing it."

"Send him on an errand," Mr. Jones suggested.

"That's a great idea. If you don't mind, I'll send him to you with a note. Just keep him for five minutes and then send him back."

"No problem, glad to help," Mr. Jones answered.

When they returned from lunch, Mrs. Garcia handed Miles an envelope with a note inside, and asked him to bring it to Mr. Jones. Miles was glad to be sent on an errand. He didn't want to hear the teasing anymore. Miles took his time getting to Mr. Jones's office

While Miles was gone, Mrs. Garcia explained to the class that Miles got upset when they teased him about his birthday.

"We didn't mean any harm," Bobby admitted.

"We didn't mean any harm," Bobby said.

"I know you didn't, but it still bothers him," said Mrs. Garcia.

"What can we do to make him happy?" asked Mary.

"How about a surprise party tomorrow?" Sean suggested.

"Yeah, he's already bringing goody bags and a cake," commented John.

"Great idea," said Mrs. Garcia. "Since we did not have art this morning, I have the perfect homework assignment. Tonight, for homework, you are to make either a gift for Miles or something for the party. In order to make this a challenge, you must use items you already have in your home. I will write a note for you to take home to your parents explaining this very unusual homework assignment. This will be your only homework tonight."

Everyone cheered at this. "Please remember, class, do not tease Miles about having his second birthday. He will be eight, just like the rest of you." The class agreed. "Also, remember: the party is a surprise!"

When Miles returned from Mr. Jones's office, the class was very excited. Miles wondered what was going on.

"John, why is everyone so excited?" Miles asked.

"We don't have any homework tonight," John answered. He did not like lying to his best friend, but this one time was necessary. He would explain tomorrow, during the party.

"Great, no homework!" shouted Miles.

They continued to learn about leap year and the calendar.

"Last week I asked you to find out two interesting things that happened on your birthday. Miles, what did you find out?"

"Well, I was the only baby born at Children's Wing Hospital on February 29 when I was born.

"Wow, that's unusual. Usually there are several babies born each day at Children's Wing Hospital. What else did you learn, Miles?" asked Mrs. Garcia.

"You're not going to believe this," said Miles "but my Great-Aunt Mamie was born on Leap Year Day, too. She is exactly 80 years older than me!"

"Two people in the same family born on Leap Year Day is very unusual," commented Mrs. Garcia.

The rest of the afternoon went by quickly. Miles wondered why he was not teased anymore, but assumed it was because everyone was excited about not having any homework.

Soon it was three o'clock and time to go home.

Chapter 4
No homework tonight!

Normally Miles goes to extended care until five-thirty, but since his mom did not go to work today, she was waiting for him at parent pick-up.

"How was school today?" she asked as Miles got into the car. She always asked this question. Usually Miles was too tired to answer, but today he was very excited and talkative.

"We learned why February only has 28 days and 29 days every four years," Miles answered.

"Really? Well, tell me!" his mom said. On the ride home Miles shared his day and the lesson about

February with his mom. He did not tell her about the teasing.

When they got home, Miles went to the kitchen for a snack of hot chocolate and ginger cookies.

On the table next to the goody bags was the birthday cake Mrs. Phillips made for his class party tomorrow. It had pink strawberry icing, which was Miles's favorite. The cake read *Happy Leap Day, Miles*, in bright red letters. Although the cake was beautiful, Miles frowned a little.

"What's wrong, Miles? Don't you like the cake?" his mom asked.

"It's great, but … but can it have an eight on it?" Miles asked.

"An eight? Of course it can. I'll put it right here," his mom said, pointing to a space on the cake. She then picked up the blue icing tube and made a big eight on the cake.

"Perfect!" exclaimed Miles. "Just perfect."

"How about getting your homework started while I make dinner?" his mom asked.

"We don't have any homework tonight," Miles replied. "No homework on a Thursday?" questioned his mom.

"Nope," Miles answered. *This is strange*, his mom thought, but she did not say anything.

While Mrs. Phillips was making dinner, the phone rang several times. Each time it was a different classmate of Miles's. They all wanted to know things about Miles, such as his favorite color, whether he liked chocolate chip cookies, if he ate vanilla pudding, and what his favorite action figure was. During dinner Mrs. Phillips asked Miles if he knew why his classmates were calling and asking these questions. Of course Miles did not know. *Something is going on,* Mrs. Phillips thought. She decided to wait until tomorrow and ask his teacher when she goes to school with the goody bags and cake.

Usually Mr. Phillips was home for dinner, but tonight he was out of town on business.

"Will Dad be home tomorrow night?" asked Miles.

"Of course, he already called me this afternoon. We can expect him in time to go out to dinner tomorrow night."

"Good," said Miles. "I have to talk to him."

Leaping Math Fun

If you were born in 1960, but has only had 10 birthdays on your birth day, how could you be 40 in the year 2000?

Answer: Because 1960 was a leap year, you must have been born on February 29. Note: See how it is worded? "on your birth day" – Leapers can only celebrate their birth day ON February 29.

If John was born on February 29, 1956 and in 2004 turned 12 leap years on his birthday, how many years old is John?

Answer: 48. The key is 12 leap years vs. how many "years" without the leap, literally!

If Carmen was born February 29, 2000, how many birthdays will she celebrate on her birthday by 2008?

Answer: 2

If Jim was born February 29, 1976, how many times did he celebrate his birthday ON his birthday by 2005?

Answer: 7. Seven times four is 28. In 2005 Jim would be 29.

Thirty days hath September,
April, June, and November;
All the rest have thirty-one,
Excepting February alone,
And it has twenty-eight days' time,
But in leap years,
February has twenty-nine.

      – Author Unknown

Friday, February 28

Thirty days hath September,
April, June, and November.
All the rest have thirty-one,
Though February's underdone
With twenty-eight–hold the line!–
Leap Day makes it twenty-nine.

                    – Author Unknown

Chapter 5
The party at school

The next morning when Miles got on the bus, he noticed that several kids in his class had an extra bag or package, including John. "What's in the box?" he asked John.

"Oh nothing, just extra lunch." *Another lie,* John said to himself. *Not a good thing.* But if he told Miles the truth, he would spoil the surprise! He would explain later, at the party.

Something is going on, Miles thought. The ride to school was extra quiet. No one teased him about being two. In fact, no one said anything about his birthday at all. Not even John and Sean. This made Miles a little sad.

After the Friday morning spelling test, the morning went quickly. Soon it was lunchtime. Mrs. Phillips was coming after lunch with the goody bags and cake.

During lunch, everyone was excited about the afternoon party. But still no one teased Miles about being two. *Now, this is really strange,* he thought. For some reason Miles did not have an appetite again. He had been sure that they would really tease him today. But they didn't.

When they returned to class, Mrs. Garcia asked Miles to take some books and a note to Mr. Jones's office. Once again Miles was being sent on an errand. But this time he did not want to go. He wanted to be there when his mom arrived. If he hurried, he could get to Mr. Jones's office and back in less than a couple of minutes! So off he went.

When he arrived at Mr. Jones's office, the assistant principal was on the phone and motioned for Miles to put the books on the desk and have a seat. By the time Mr. Jones got off the phone and read the note, then wrote another note back to Mrs. Garcia, fifteen minutes had gone by.

Miles raced back down the hall to his classroom. When he got there, he noticed that the door was shut.

What's going on? Miles wondered. The door was only closed during tests. When Miles opened the door, everyone yelled, "Happy Birthday, Miles!"

Miles was so shocked he dropped the note for Mrs. Garcia. The first thing Miles saw was his mom standing next to the cake, and then he saw the mountain of gifts and balloons on his desk. In fact, there were balloons everywhere!

"Where did these come from?" asked Miles.

"We made them for you," said John excitedly.

"So that's what was in the box you had this morning," remarked Miles to John. "I knew it wasn't lunch." John just smiled. He was glad that his friend figured it out.

"Our homework assignment was to make something for you for your birthday," Sean said. Now Mrs. Phillips knew why the kids were calling the house last night.

"I made you chocolate lollipops. My mother helped me last night," Carmen told Miles.

"I made you a picture frame," Mary said. "The fabric has the number eight on it."

"Wow, this is great, Mary!" said Miles. One by one, Miles opened all the gifts. He thought he was the luckiest kid in the world.

"Okay, class," Mrs. Garcia said. "Mrs. Phillips has baked a cake for this special occasion, and look – the cake has eight candles!"

All the children, Mrs. Garcia, and Mrs. Phillips sang *Happy Birthday* to Miles. Then Miles made a wish and blew out the candles. Mrs. Phillips cut the cake and gave everyone a big piece and their goody bags.

What a great party, Mrs. Garcia thought, *and no one called Miles two years old.* Just then the classroom door burst open and Mr. Watson, the school principal, came in. "Happy second birthday, Miles!" he yelled. "I've waited all year to say that!" He laughed and left with a piece of cake.

No sooner had he left than Miss Waller, the new librarian, arrived. She was carrying two small packages wrapped in sports wrapping paper.

"These are for you, Miles," said Miss Waller.

"Wow, two gifts. Thanks, Miss Waller!" exclaimed Miles.

"Yes, one for each year," she laughed, while reaching for a piece of cake. Although Miles was glad to get two gifts from Miss Waller, there was a slight sadness to his smile. Both Mrs. Garcia and Mrs. Phillips noticed how much this bothered Miles. The kids in the class noticed, too.

"Don't worry, Miles, we all know that you will be eight tomorrow," Karen told Miles. But that didn't matter. During the rest of the afternoon, it seemed like the entire school knew that Miles was having his second birthday tomorrow. The basketball coach, the crossing guard, the lunch cook, his kindergarten teacher Mrs. McCaffery, the Spanish teacher and even Mr. Johnson the janitor all managed to find the time to stop by Mrs. Garcia's class and wish Miles a happy second birthday.

By the end of the day, Miles had gone from glad to sad. The only person who visited the class and wished him a happy eighth birthday was Mr. Jones. Mr. Jones handed Miles a large birthday card. The card had two singing frogs on it, and it said *"Happy Birthday, February 29, Leap Year Day."*

"Wow, this card is great, Mr. Jones!" shouted Miles.

"I'm glad you like it, Miles. When I saw it at the store last night I immediately thought of you," Mr. Jones replied.

This made Miles feel a lot better.

Leap Year Facts

Leap Seconds

Some years are longer than others. Every few years, scientists agree to add or remove a second from a year right at midnight on December 31st. This is called a Leap Second.

Leap Moons

Many countries use a lunar calendar to celebrate religious holidays. Whenever the lunar calendar falls behind the solar calendar by more than a moon month, a Leap Moon Month is added to the lunar calendar.

Leap Year comes every 4 years.
If the year ends in double zero (00) it must be divisible by 400 in order to be a Leap Year.
Therefore, 1900 was not a Leap Year.
2100 & 2200 will not be Leap Years.

But,
2000 was a Leap Year
and 2400 will be a Leap Year.

Thirty days hath November,
April, June, and September,
February hath xxviii alone,
And all the rest have xxxi.

— Richard Grafton:
Chronicles of England (1590)

Chapter 6
A leap year tradition

On the ride home, Miles described the events of the afternoon to his mom as though she had not been there. Halfway home Miles became very quiet. Finally he asked his mom, "Why do people think I'm going to be two? Don't they understand that it's my *second birthday date*, but I am really going to be eight?"

"Sure, they understand that. But traditionally, when a person is born on Leap Year Day, they are teased about the number of years they have had a birthday date. Yours is two."

"I don't like this tradition," Miles said sadly.

Finally they arrived home. In the driveway was Miles's father's black car. "Is Dad home already?" Miles asked.

"It looks like it," said his mom.

"Good! I'll talk to him, he'll understand," Miles said as he got out of the car.

Just then the front door opened and out came Miles's dad. Since Miles had a party at school, Mr. Phillips yelled, "Happy Second Birthday!" with a big smile and arms stretched ready for a big hug. He thought this would be in keeping with the spirit from the party at school. Without a word, Miles just ran past him and into the house. Miles didn't even stop to pet Einstein who was waiting patiently at the door with his tail a-wagging. Einstein looked after Miles for a second then ran behind him. *Maybe this is a new game,* thought Einstein.

"What happened at school today?" Mr. Phillips asked Mrs. Phillips. "Wasn't the party a huge success?"

"Yes, the party was great," Mrs. Phillips said. Then she explained to Mr. Phillips about the special gifts Miles's classmates made for him, the cake and all the visitors. She also explained how Miles felt about being teased about his second birthday.

"Well, I sure messed that up, didn't I?" remarked Mr. Phillips.

"It's not your fault. You didn't know. Don't worry about it. As soon as we get to Don's Big Rib House for dinner, Miles will forget all about it."

"I guess you're right," Mr. Phillips said. "Here, let me help you bring in all the gifts. Is there any leftover cake?" he asked hopefully.

"Oh, yes, I made sure I brought home a piece for dessert tonight," Mrs. Phillips answered.

Mr. and Mrs. Phillips took all the gifts from the car and brought them into the house. Miles was sitting at the kitchen table with his head down. Mr. Phillips went to the refrigerator and poured two glasses of iced tea. He gave one to Miles and sat next to him while Mrs. Phillips was organizing the gifts.

"You know, Miles, your Great-Aunt Mamie was born on Leap Year Day, too. She will be 88 years old tomorrow," his dad said.

"Yeah, I know," Miles said without much enthusiasm.

"Why don't you call her tonight and say happy birthday, since she will not be coming to the party tomorrow?"

"That's a wonderful idea!" said his mom. She was already dialing the number. "Here, Miles, the phone is ringing." Miles took the phone from his mom. It rang two more times before Aunt Mamie answered.

"Hello, and happy birthday to me," sang Aunt Mamie into the phone.

"Hi, Aunt Mamie, it's me, Miles," said Miles.

"Miles … you mean Leap Year Day Miles? You mean my great-nephew that has the same birthday as me, Miles?" Aunt Mamie asked teasingly.

"Yeah that's the one," answered Miles, playing along. "Your birthday is not until tomorrow. Why are you answering the phone *happy birthday to me* today?" asked Miles.

"I'm practicing," said Aunt Mamie.

Miles thought about this for a moment, and then asked, "How does it feel to be almost 88 years old?"

"88 years old?" asked Aunt Mamie. "I would not know, because I'm going to be 22 years old tomorrow."

Just then, Aunt Mamie's doorbell rang. "I'm expecting company for dinner. Gotta go. Thanks for calling, Miles. And you have a happy birthday, too."

Click. She was gone. Miles handed the phone back to his mom with a bewildered look.

"What's wrong, Miles?" his mom asked.

"I don't think Aunt Mamie is well."

"Not well?" asked his dad with concern. "Did she sound sick?"

"No, just kinda weird," said Miles.

"Then why do you think she is not well" his dad asked.

"Because she thinks she's going to be 22 years old tomorrow," replied Miles, exasperation in his voice.

"Oh," laughed his dad. "Well, in a way, she is."

"Well, she can be 22 if she wants to, but I'm going to be eight!" stormed Miles as he ran from the kitchen. Of course Einstein was right behind him. *I guess we're playing that game again,* thought Einstein.

Mr. and Mrs. Phillips looked at each other. They each wondered what to do about this. Tomorrow is Miles's birthday, and he should be happy… not sad.

"Being born on Leap Year Day is an exciting and wonderful birthday," Mrs. Phillips said to Mr. Phillips.

"Yes, it is. But being eight is also wonderful," remarked Mr. Phillips.

Miles was so upset that he ran right past all the decorations without noticing them. There were balloons, party hats, party favors, and a box of prizes for all the games they were going to play. The furniture had been moved around and another cake was on the counter in the kitchen.

Mrs. Phillips went to find Miles. She decided not to mention the situation. They could talk about it later after dinner if Miles was still upset. He was lying on his bed in his room. "You know, Miles, around 60 people will be coming tomorrow for your birthday party," his mom said.

"Sixty?" Miles repeated, trying to sound upset.

"Yeah, so let's go to dinner and get back here early so we can get things ready for tomorrow," his dad said from the doorway of Miles's bedroom. "Your mom has a lot to do and she needs our help."

"Where are we going for dinner?" asked Miles.

"Oh, we're going to your favorite restaurant," his mom answered.

"Don's Big Rib House … here we come! Are we still picking up John and Sean?" asked Miles.

"They will meet us there," his mom replied "Their families are coming, too!"

"Hot diggity dog, let's go!" yelled Miles while jumping off his bed.

As Miles was on his way to the front door, he noticed the cake on the counter in the kitchen. "Wow, Mom," said Miles, "this cake is bigger than the one you made for school today!" Although he did not mention it, Miles noticed the large red eight in the middle of the cake, and of course it had pink strawberry icing! This made him feel very happy. When Miles looked up from the table he noticed all the party decorations in the living room.

"Come on, Miles, let's go!" yelled his dad from the door. "We're going to be late." Miles took a second more to look at all the party stuff and cake, and then ran to the front door with a big smile. Things were going to be great. This was his best birthday ever!

They had to wait a few minutes for Mrs. Phillips to find her purse. She said she had misplaced it.

Chapter 7
Dinner with family and friends

The ride to the restaurant was peaceful and quiet, mainly because Miles fell asleep in the backseat. Mr. and Mrs. Phillips enjoyed the peace and quiet.

"Wake up, Miles, we're here," his dad announced as they pulled into the restaurant parking lot.

"What? We're here? Good, I'm starving," Miles said as he jumped out of the car and ran toward his friends who were waiting outside the restaurant. Don's Big Rib House was crowded, but since they had a reservation they did not have to wait.

Miles and Sean did not have any brothers or sisters, but John had two younger brothers. So they were eleven in all. With eleven people, you got to sit in the private room. The room was big enough for about twenty-five people, so it was like having a private party. There was one group of twelve already there.

Miles loved Don's Big Rib House because it was all you could eat ribs, all the time.

After everyone ordered, the boys talked about the events of the past two days. Mr. and Mrs. Phillips were happy to see that Miles could talk about it without getting upset.

Since Miles had not eaten his lunch earlier, he was very hungry. He ate a full rack of ribs and a load of curly fries with cheese and hot sauce. Miles loved hot sauce.

"Boy, Miles, you were hungry," commented his mom.

"Yeah," smiled Miles remembering that he did not eat his lunch. "I was, but I'm full now."

The dinner was perfect. No one called Miles two. "When do you celebrate Miles's birthday when it is not leap year?" Sean's mother asked Mrs. Phillips.

"Oh, we sometimes celebrate on February twenty-eighth and sometimes on March first," answered Mrs.

Phillips, "but on a leap year we definitely celebrate on the twenty-ninth."

"Hey, did you know that Miles is a *Leaper?*" yelled John across the table to his mother.

"A what?" asked Miles.

"A *Leaper*. I almost forgot. I found this really cool list of Leap terms called *The Leaptionary* on the Internet. I made a couple of copies," John said while getting the list out of his pocket. "See, here it says '*Leaper—A person born on Leap Day.*' There are other great words, too."

"Let me see?" asked Miles.

John gave Miles a copy. "Hey, Dad I'm a *Leaper,* and you and Mom are *Leapless*. That's anyone not born on February twenty-ninth."

For the next half-hour everyone kept naming people who fit the various leap-categories. At eight o'clock Mrs. Phillips announced that it was getting late and they had a lot of things to finish that night before the party tomorrow.

"Just ten more minutes Mom, please," begged Miles.

"Okay, just ten more, and then we must be going."

Finally, at eight-fifteen, they were all in their cars heading home.

Again the car ride was peaceful and quiet. Miles had fallen asleep. "Boy, he's very tired today," commented Mr. Phillips.

"I think it's all the excitement about his birthday," said Mrs. Phillips. "It's burned him out a little. Let's just put him to bed, and we can finish up for tomorrow."

"I'm glad no one said anything about this being his second birthday tonight." said Mr. Phillips.

"Oh, I made sure of that," said Mrs. Phillips. "While you and Miles were waiting in the car for me to find my purse, I was calling John's and Sean's parents to explain the situation."

"That was smart," said Mr. Phillips.

When they got home, they didn't wake Miles. Mr. Phillips just carried him and put him to bed, clothes and all, except for his sneakers.

The Leaptionary

Leaper – a person born on Leap Day

Leapeans – people born on Leap Day

Leapless – anyone *not* born on Leap Day

Leapling – a newborn Leap Day baby

Leapette – female Leapean

Leapster – male Leapean

Leapingly yours – as in "sincerely yours"

Leapest Regards – something that is delicious

Leap Couple – two Leapies married to each other

Leapship – friendship between Leap Day babies

Leap On! – "Right On" between Leap Day babies

Saturday, February 29

Leap Year Day

Thirty days hath September,
April, June, and November;
All the rest have thirty-one
Except February alone:
Which has twenty-eight three years in four,
Till Leap Year gives it just one more.

– Author Unknown

Chapter 8
The party
Leap Year Day is here!

The party was planned for twelve o'clock. Yet at nine-thirty, when Miles finally woke up, the house was filled with people and already smelled like dinner.

"Oh, you finally woke up, birthday boy," said his mom from the doorway, looking into his room.

"What time is it?" asked Miles through a yawn.

"It's nine-thirty. John and Sean have already called. They want to come over early, so they are on their way. While you take a shower, I'll get your breakfast and bring it to you. You can eat in your room today, just this once, because there is no room in the kitchen. The house is already filled with people."

"Yeah, I can hear all the noise. Who's here?" asked Miles.

"Well, let's see. Big Mama and Granddaddy are here."

"Did Big Mama bring the bread pudding?" asked Miles hopefully.

"Of course, a big one, and Granddaddy made his famous BBQ sauce for the chicken. Your cousin Wayne is here too, and wait until you see the great banner he made for you! It's hung over the front door. Oh, I almost forgot. Your Aunt Rose is also here, and she's making her ice cream punch."

"Ice cream punch?" repeated Miles.

"Yeah, you know, the one you drank too much of at Christmas."

"Oooh, yeah," Miles said as he remembered the stomachache he had sufferd through later that evening. "It was really good."

"And some of your cousins are here, too."

While Miles was in the shower Mrs. Phillips put his breakfast in the room. Blueberry waffles and a glass of strawberry milk.

Miles was too excited to eat. But Einstein was always hungry. Miles put his plate on the floor for Einstein while keeping one eye on the door, making sure his mom didn't catch him. Einstein was very happy. A whole plate of blueberry waffles. It must be his lucky day. The waffles were gone in less than a minute. Miles drank the strawberry milk.

Miles dressed quickly and headed downstairs. By now it was ten o'clock.

There were balloons everywhere and a big sign hung over the front door that said *Happy Birthday, Miles – It's Leap Year Day.*

Just then the front door opened and in came Uncle Wes.

"Happy birthday, nephew!" Uncle Wes called in his usual bubbly baritone voice. "How does it feel to be two? Man, you sure are big for being two!" Uncle Wes was so busy laughing that he didn't notice the look on Miles's face as he ran to the kitchen.

"What's wrong, Miles?" asked Big Mama when he entered the kitchen.

"Nothing," said Miles, trying to act happy. *Hopefully only Uncle Wes will call me two,* Miles thought.

John and Sean and their families arrived around ten-thirty. Miles was glad to see them.

John and Sean brought Miles new video games, which they immediately attacked in his bedroom. Miles was glad to get away, because it seemed like everyone at the party called him *two* or said something about *two*.

A little while later Mrs. Phillips went to find the boys. "Miles, you guys have been in here long enough. It's time for you to come back downstairs and join the party," his mom said. "I'll give you fifteen more minutes, and then I expect to see the three of you downstairs with the rest of the guests." Miles dreaded going back downstairs.

In exactly fifteen minutes Miles, John and Sean descended the stairs and rejoined the party. Everyone one was happy to see the birthday boy. A lot more people were there now. No one called him two. Miles relaxed and enjoyed his birthday party. They played lots of games, danced, and ate. Boy did they eat!

Miles counted five different types of chicken: BBQ chicken, fried chicken, grilled chicken with mushroom sauce, honey-glazed chicken wings, and chicken cutlets. Miles loved chicken so he tried some of each. They were all great. Along with the five different types of chicken were two different salads. One had baby greens and mandarin oranges and the other was a spinach salad with walnuts. Miles did not have to guess who brought the salads. It was most definitely Aunt Betty – or Aunt Salad, as Miles secretly called her.

At five o'clock Mrs. Phillips announced that it was time to cut the cake.

"Hey, Miles!" yelled Uncle Wes from the corner, "Are you going to sing *I'm two years old* now?" Miles tried to ignore this but several people began to ask the same question as Mrs. Phillips carried out the cake.

The cake was perfect, with eight candles and a big red eight in the middle. Everyone sang "Happy birthday" to Miles. Then they sang "How old are you now?" Several people held up two fingers like the peace sign while singing. Miles tried to ignore them. Then it became his time to sing … and did he sing!

"I'm eight years old now. I was born on Leap Year Day. This is my second birthday, but I'm eight years old now."

Everyone cheered!

Mr. and Mrs. Phillips were both so proud of Miles they gave him a great big hug. The party continued well into the early evening.

Although Miles enjoyed his party, he couldn't help but wonder what day he would celebrate his birthday next year. After asking his mom two previous times, she finally had an answer for him the third time. "You can pick whatever day you want to celebrate your birthday next year."

"Really!" Miles exclaimed. "Any day?'

"That's right, any day you choose," his mom replied with a big smile. *That ought to keep him thinking,* she thought as she walked away, leaving a happy little boy to his thoughts.

Soon it was nine o'clock and everyone began leaving.

When Uncle Wes was leaving, he yelled from the door with a big laugh, "See you in four years, Miles ... when you're *three*." Several of the guests started saying it too as they were leaving, and everyone was laughing.

Mr. and Mrs. Phillips looked at Miles with worried frowns.

"Well, I guess I'd better get used to it," Miles said to his parents with a smile. "Hey! Maybe I'll get *three* presents from everyone next time for being three!"

Leap Year & Calendar Facts
Source Credits

Pages 18, 25, 46, 48,
55, 56, 69, 72
The Honor Society of Leap Day Babies
www.leapzine.com

Page 26
Togodumnus/Kevan White
http://www.roman-britain.org/

Pages 33 & 34
Reprinted courtesy
The Minneapolis Institute of Arts

What would you do if you were told that you could pick any day you want to celebrate your birthday?

What day would you choose?

Introduction
February 29th does not come this year!

It's January first, just past seven-thirty in the morning. Miles wakes up with a very slow start, but as soon as his eyes open and focus he remembers... it's not leap year this year! *What a bummer,* he thinks, because he always gets lots of extra gifts on leap year.

Next to his bed is the scrapbook his mom made for him from his leap year birthday parties last year. As he looks through the pages and laughs and smiles at all the memories, he soon recalls the promise his mom made and a smile comes to his face.

Three times during his party last year, he asked her, "What day will we celebrate my birthday next year?" The first two times she just smiled, thinking. Then on the third time she said the most perfect sentence a child could ever hear: *"You can pick whatever day you want to celebrate your birthday next year."*

What day should he pick? February twenty-eighth, March first, or another day? He was not sure. Suddenly he realized that this sentence, although perfect, was full of complications and decisions. *It is so much easier during a leap year,* he thought. The date was picked for him. February twenty-ninth, the day he was born. "Wait a minute!" he said out loud to no one. "I have this problem for the next three years!" If only the non-leap years were every four years instead!

About the Author

Being the mother of a Leap Year Day child
inspired Michelle to write this story.

On February 29, 1996, Michelle's son Miles
turned eight. For his birthday, Michelle wanted
to buy him a children's story book
about leap year.
To her surprise, she could not find one.
Making a note of this, Michelle began to outline
It's My Birthday... Finally! A Leap Year Story.

Although written for children,
Michelle's intent is to teach
as well as to entertain.

Michelle currently resides in New Jersey.

Michelle is also the author of the book
*Yours, Mine & God's: Giving and Receiving
All for the Love of God and the Church*

For Leap Year Gifts and Apparel visit

www.cafepress.com/Leap_Year

To order by mail

Hobby House Publishing Group, Inc.
P.O. Box 1527
Jackson, NJ 08527

It's My Birthday... Finally!
A Leap Year Story

Please include $10.95 per book,
plus $4.00 shipping for the first book, and $.50 cents
shipping for each additional copy.

Order on line at
www.hobbyhousepublishinggroup.com

New Leap Year workbook
by Michelle W. Winfrey

Coming soon!

Lightning Source UK Ltd.
Milton Keynes UK
UKHW011153100220
358475UK00002B/744

9 780972 717953